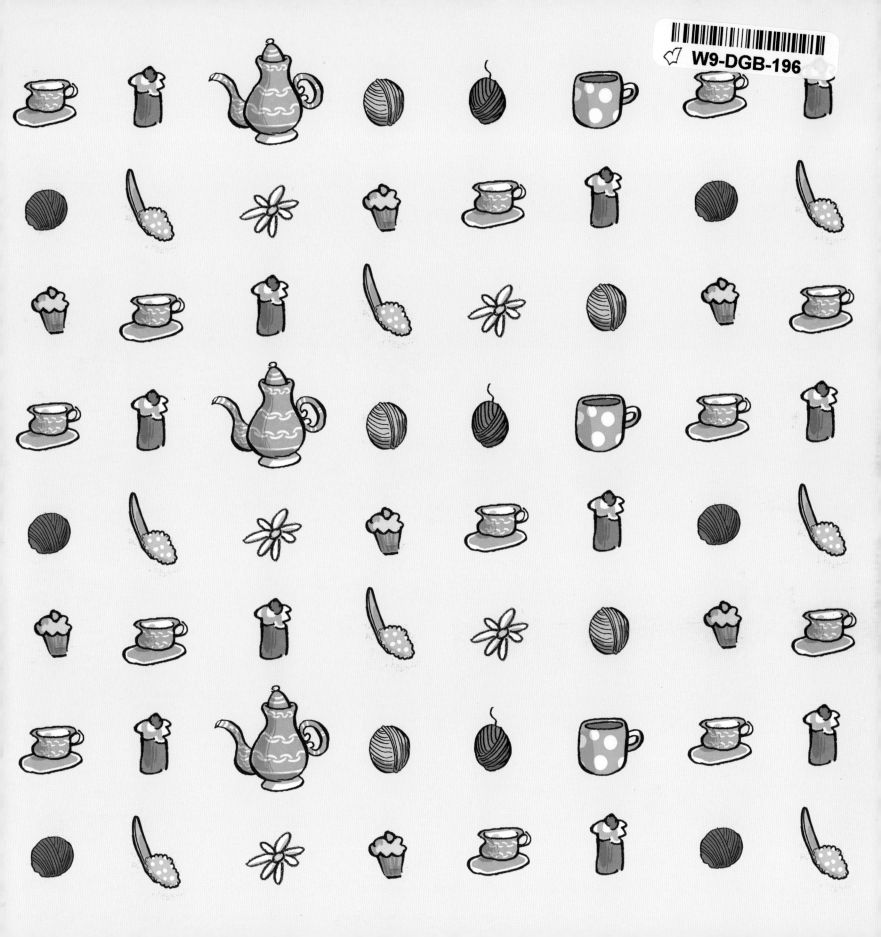

This book belongs to:

....

little bee books

An imprint of Bonnier Publishing Group
853 Broadway, New York, New York 10003
Copyright © 2015 by Igloo Books Ltd
This little bee books edition, 2016.
All rights reserved, including the right of
reproduction in whole or in part in any form.
LITTLE BEE BOOKS is a trademark of
Bonnier Publishing Group, and
associated colophon is a trademark of
Bonnier Publishing Group.

Manufactured in China HUN001 0116
First Edition 2 4 6 8 10 9 7 5 3 1
Library of Congress Cataloging-in-
Publication Data is available upon request.
ISBN 978-1-4998-0257-3

littlebeebooks.com
bonnierpublishing.com

What Pirates Really Do

by Melanie Joyce ILLUSTRATED by Alex Paterson

little bee books

Oh,
it's such a **jolly** life
for **pirates**...

...sailing on the sea!

It's even **jollier** still when it's time to go **home** for **tea!**

There are **swashbuckling** island adventures...

...and chests chock-full of **gold**.

There are **soft** and **cuddly** knitting classes...

...when the weather's cold.

By day, the pirates sail their ship...

...and **raid** along the coast.

But **relaxing** in the evenings
is what they like **the most.**

...and live on salty snails.

Back at home, they put on pajamas...

...and read their **favorite tales.**

Sometimes other **fierce** pirates come along…

...to pick a
fight.

Then everyone goes home, snuggles up...